ALL the MUCHOS in the WORLD

A Story about Love

Pauline
BOOKS & MEDIA
Boston

Library of Congress Cataloging-in-Publication Data

Carson, Diana Pastora.
   All the muchos in the world : a story about love / written by Diana Pastora Carson ; illustrated by Ginny Pruitt.
         p. cm.
   Summary: Ana discovers that her family loves her very much, but God loves her even more. A parrot in the margin translates the many Spanish words that appear throughout the text.
   ISBN 0-8198-0779-6 (pbk.)
   [1. Love—Fiction. 2. Family life—Fiction. 3. Spanish language—Fiction. 4. Hispanic Americans—Fiction. 5. Christian life—Fiction.]   I. Pruitt, Ginny, ill. II. Title.
   PZ7.C2384Al 2006
   [E]—dc22

                                                        2005016974

Published by Pauline Books & Media, 50 Saint Paul's Avenue, Boston, MA 02130-3491.

Printed in Canada

www.pauline.org

Pauline Books & Media is the publishing house of the Daughters of St. Paul, an international congregation of women religious serving the Church with the communications media.

1 2 3 4 5 6 7 8 9   11 10 09 08 07 06

Ana loved her family. She loved her *abuela* and *abuelo*. She loved her *mamá,* her *papá,* and her *hermanito*. Ana even bragged about how much she loved them.

Something to learn!
Something to learn!
Abuela means *grandmother* in Spanish.
Abuelo means *grandfather*.
Hermanito means *little brother*.

Ana's *familia* loved her too. But could they really love her as much as she loved them? Ana didn't think so. She didn't think anyone could feel as much love as she felt in her *corazón*.

Can you guess what *familia* means? *Corazón* means *heart*. *Corazón* means *heart*.

5

One morning, Ana had an idea.... She ran to find her father. "*Papá,*" she asked, "*¿cuánto me quieres?* How much do you love me?" Ana's *papá* grinned. He put down the towel he was folding and picked up Ana. "I love you a whole lot," he answered.

Next, Ana went to look for her mother. "*Mamá, ¿cuánto me quieres?* How much do you love me?" Her *mamá* put down her spoon. "Ana," she said with a smile, "a mother's love is so great that it can't be measured."

7

Then Ana went to find her grandmother. "*Abuela,
¿cuánto me quieres?* How much do you love me?"
Ana asked.

"*Mija, ¡yo te quiero mucho!*" her grandmother
proudly said as she made Ana's hair look pretty. "My
child, I love you very much!"

8

Ana's grandfather was watching. "*Abuelo, ¿cuánto me quieres?*" Ana asked him.

"Ana, *¡yo te quiero muchísimo!*" her grandfather exclaimed.

Wow! Ana thought. *That's even more than mucho!*

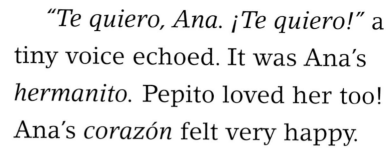

"*Te quiero, Ana. ¡Te quiero!*" a tiny voice echoed. It was Ana's *hermanito*. Pepito loved her too! Ana's *corazón* felt very happy.

¡Te quiero!
I love you!
Corazón means *heart*.
¡Te quiero!
I love you!
Corazón means *heart*.

10

Now Ana knew how much everyone in her family loved her. But she was still sure that she loved them *mucho más,* so much more. She still thought that her love was bigger than everyone else's.

11

Ana was proud of herself. She was eager to share her love with her *familia*. She had to find her father before he left for work!

Ana's father was just getting into the car. *"Papá, do you know how much I love you?"* Ana asked. "How much?" her father answered in surprise. Ana's brown eyes sparkled. She smiled her biggest smile and stretched her arms out wide.

Then she went dancing down the driveway singing, *"¡Mucho! ¡Mucho, mucho, mucho, mucho, mucho, mucho, mucho, mucho, mucho, mucho, mucho, mucho, mucho, mucho, mucho, mucho!…"* until she was completely out of breath.

Mucho means very much! Mucho means very much!

13

Ana did the same thing to her *mamá* and to her *abuela*. She did it to her *abuelo* and her *hermanito* too. "*¡Mucho! ¡Mucho, mucho, mucho, mucho, mucho, mucho, mucho, mucho, mucho, mucho, mucho, mucho, mucho, mucho, mucho!*" Ana sang as she danced through the house. Why was Ana acting like this? Pepito wasn't sure. But Ana was sure that her love was much bigger than any love in the whole wide world!

Pepito is Ana's *hermanito!*
Pepito is Ana's *hermanito!*

15

That evening, Ana's *abuela*, *abuelo*, *mamá*, *papá*, and *hermanito* got together. They came up with a plan. They decided what they would do the next time Ana asked, *"¿Cuánto me quieres?"*

16

The next day was Saturday, one of Ana's favorite days. That afternoon, Ana wanted to hear about her *familia's* love again.

Ana found her father in the back yard. *"Papá,"* she asked him, *"¿cuánto me quieres?"* Her *papá* shut off the lawn mower. "Not ¡*mucho, mucho, mucho, mucho, mucho, mucho, mucho, mucho, mucho, mucho, mucho, mucho, mucho, mucho, mucho, mucho, mucho, mucho, mucho, mucho!*" he said. "I love you even more than that…*mucho más.*" Then Ana's *papá* smiled his biggest smile and stretched his arms out wide. "I love you all the *muchos* in the world!" he exclaimed.

18

¿Cuánto me quieres?
How much do you love me?

19

Oh, my child!
Oh, my child!

Ana took a deep breath. She hurried over to her mother. *"Mamá, ¿cuánto me quieres?"* she asked.

"Oh, *mija*," her mother replied, "if you could count every grain of sand on all the beaches in the world, you would not even come close to the amount of *muchos* that make up how much I love you."

Ana's *mamá* put down her groceries. Then she smiled her biggest smile and stretched her arms out wide. "I love you all the *muchos* in the world!" she exclaimed.

Ana chuckled as she skipped over to her grandmother. *"Abuela,"* she asked, *"¿cuánto me quieres?"*

Ana's grandmother looked down at the blanket she was knitting, and then up at Ana. "Do you see the many stitches that make up this blanket? If I could make a blanket big enough to keep the whole world warm, and if you could count each stitch in that blanket, their number could not match the amount of *muchos* there are in my love for you." Then Ana's *abuela* smiled her biggest smile and stretched her arms out wide. "I love you all the *muchos* in the world!" she exclaimed.

Ana excitedly ran to her grandfather and little brother. *"Abuelo,"* she asked, *"¿cuánto me quieres?"*

"Oh, precious child," he answered, "if you were to count all the *muchos* that fit into my *corazón* for you, it would take more than your entire lifetime." Her *abuelo* winked at Ana's *hermanito*. Then Ana's *abuelo* smiled his biggest smile and stretched his arms out wide. "I love you all the *muchos* in the world!" he exclaimed.

"¡Te quiero!" Pepito squealed. "I love you!"

Ana's *corazón* felt so very happy.

Corazón means *heart.*
Corazón means *heart.*

24

That night, when it was time for bed, Ana gave good-night *besos* to her *papá* and *mamá*. She gave kisses to her *abuela, abuelo,* and *hermanito* too. The kisses she got back were as full of love as any kisses could be. *Maybe my* familia *does love me even more than I love them,* Ana thought. Her *familia's* love felt like it was the biggest love in the whole wide world!

27

28

Ana knelt beside her bed. She closed her eyes to say her prayers. She thanked God for her loving *familia*. She told God that she loved him. But before Ana said, "*Amén*," she asked God her important question: "*¿Diós, cuánto me quieres?*"

Diós means *God*.
Diós means *God*.

29

Then Ana opened her eyes. She looked up and saw the cross hanging above her bed. She saw that Jesus had his arms stretched out wide. Right then, Ana knew that there was a love greater and bigger than her love and greater and bigger than her family's love. In her *corazón,* Ana knew that God's love for each one of us is the greatest and biggest love in the whole wide world!!! Ana smiled her biggest smile. *"Gracias, Diós,"* she whispered. "Thank you, God, for loving me even more than all the *muchos* in the world…*mucho más."*

Pronunciation Guide and Glossary

abuela — (ah-buéh-lah) grandmother

abuelo — (ah-buéh-lō) grandfather

amor — (ah-mór) love

corazón — (cō-rah-zón) heart

Diós — (Deeós) God

familia — (fah-meé-lee-ah) family

gracias — (gráh-seeahs) thank you

hermano — (er-máh-nō) brother

hermanito — (er-mah-née-tō) little brother

mamá — (mah-máh) mother

más — (máhs) more

mija — (méeha) my child

muchísimo — (moo-cheé-see-mō) very much or a whole lot

mucho — (moó-chō) much or a lot

papá — (pah-páh) father

Te quiero — (teh kyéh-rō) I love you

Yo te quiero mucho — (Yō teh kyéh-rō moó-chō)
I love you very much